The Pirate Queen

TERRY DEARY'S
PIRATE TALES

The Pirate Queen

Illustrated by Helen Flook

A & C Black • London

First published 2011 by
A & C Black Publishers Ltd
36 Soho Square, London, W1D 3QY

www.acblack.com

Text copyright © 2011 Terry Deary
Illustrations copyright © 2011 Helen Flook

ISBN 978-1-4081-2835-0

A CIP catalogue for this book is available from the British Library.

This book is produced using paper that is made from wood grown in
managed, sustainable forests. It is natural, renewable and recyclable.
The logging and manufacturing processes conform to the
environmental regulations of the country of origin.

Printed and bound in Great Britain
by CPI Cox & Wyman, Reading RG1 8EX.

Chapter One
Bald and Bold

Ireland, 1593

My ma was the greatest pirate that ever lived. My ma was the terror of the Irish Sea. My ma made strong men turn to water.

My ma was Grace O'Malley.

How do I know she was the greatest terror that ever turned water into pirates... I mean the greatest pirate that ever turned the Irish Sea into water... I mean... oh, you know what I mean.

How do I know she was great? Because she told me. She told me every day she was back home.

"Catherine," she said. "Catherine, your ma is the greatest pirate that ever lived."

"Are you really, Ma?" I asked and looked up at her fine figure with her cropped, red hair. Her hair was so short they called her Granuaile in the old Irish language. If you're not Irish, that means 'bald'. (If you *are* Irish, it still means 'bald'.)

Most girls are proud of their mothers and think they're as pretty as a shamrock in bloom. Now, even when I was too young to walk, I knew my ma wasn't a beauty. Her face was blotched by the salty west winds and scarred with fifty fights. Her nose was broken and one eye was half blind.

But I was still proud of my ma, Grace O'Malley. Of course I wanted to be just like her. I wanted to bring back riches to our castle in Connacht. If you're not Irish, then you need to know that Connacht is the grandest county in Ireland. (If you *are* Irish, it's still a grand county on the west coast of Ireland... and I don't care how grand you think *your* county might be, I'll fight anyone who says Connacht's not the best.)

As I say, I wanted to be just like my ma. I wanted to be a pirate. The problem was

I could not wait. And that's how I got into all that trouble.

Mind you, it was just as well I did cause that trouble, because it was me who saved the life of Grace O'Malley, Pirate Queen of Connacht.

I remember the night we sat in the great hall of the castle. The chill wind blew wild around Clare Island and all the shutters

in Ireland couldn't keep it out. Even the blazing log fire didn't warm the room very much. My ma and her captains sat close to the fire. The poor peasants and the children like me shivered in the draughty dim corners with the dogs.

The last crumb of bread was eaten and the last bit of mutton gristle spat on the floor and Grace O'Malley filled her wine cup. "Here's good luck to the pirates of Connacht!" she cried. "And may the seas be full of treasure ships tomorrow!"

The captains cheered and the sailors on the benches waved their hats. In the corners we coughed and sniffled.

"Tell us a story, Queen Grace!" a sailor shouted.

Of course she wasn't a real queen, just the leader of the O'Malley clan, but the pitiless pirates of Clare Island would follow her to the death. That's what mattered.

"A story?" she smiled. "I don't know any stories."

The men laughed. "Tell us about when you were a wee girl," old Hugh O'Neil called out.

"Aye!" the others cried. They settled down with their warm wine and turned to face their pirate queen.

And so she began...

Chapter Two
Sea and Swords

"When I was a girl," Grace said, "my mother wanted me to be a lady. She taught me sewing and mending, painting and playing the lute, curling my long red hair in ringlets and making perfume from rose petals. I was so *bored* I could have jumped off the top of Clare Castle tower!"

"Hurrah!" the pirates cheered.

"I begged my father to take me with him on his next trip to Spain, but he said he wouldn't dare... my mother would kill him!"

"Haaaa!" the pirates laughed.

"So I cut off my hair, stole clothes from a serving boy, and went down to the harbour. I walked over the gangplank to my father's galley and told a sailor I was the new cabin boy.

"I hid in a cabin till the ship was far out to sea and then I slipped away and found my father."

"Ooooh!" the pirates sighed, knowing what a fierce temper the old chief had.

"First he said he'd throw me over the side to feed the fishes. But I told him I was too skinny to feed a minnow. He laughed and said I could stay, but if he attacked another ship, I had to go below deck. And so I sailed to Spain with my father's fleet of four galleys."

"Hurrah!"

"One morning the lookout sighted an English cog and the crew raced to clear the decks. Father was too busy to notice me on the forecastle. That cog was as slow as a donkey in the water and we soon caught up with her, threw grappling lines across and made ready to climb aboard."

"Ooooh!"

"But what Father didn't know was the cog had a troop of English soldiers aboard, and instead of us jumping aboard them, *they* jumped onto our decks."

"Ahhhh!"

"Swords flashed and muskets blasted. I didn't want to be trapped in a cabin with no way out. So I climbed the rigging ropes that hung from the main mast and watched them fighting down below. Slowly, the English drove back our crew, and my father was facing an evil English soldier..."

"Down with the English," the pirates muttered.

"Then my father's sword snapped. He was helpless. The English soldier raised his weapon to split my father's skull in two. And that's when I jumped from the rigging, landed on the enemy's sword arm and saved my father's life.

"Father picked up the sword and gave a mighty scream. Aieeee! He led the men forward and drove the English into the sea."

"Hurrah!"

"And from that time on I was a member of the crew. And now I am your leader."

The men roared and drank and others stood up to tell their tales. But it was the *start* of Ma's story that *I* remembered. That's what kept me awake that night under my sheepskin cloak... not just the cold. And that's why I did what I did the next day...

Chapter Three
Rats and Ropes

The October dawn was damp and drizzly. Most dawns are on the west coast of Ireland. The men in our pirate crew hurried to their ships with heads down and backs loaded with food sacks and water barrels, weapons and tools.

The ship smelled of tar where the planks had been patched to keep the grey waters out. I stepped onto the shaking gangplank. Or maybe it was a steady gangplank and it was my *legs* that were shaking. No one tried to stop me. I darted into the cabin on the stern deck and waited in the dark with only a family of rats for company.

At last, I felt the ship begin to move and the old oak timbers creak as they twisted in the waves. Feet ran over the decks, ropes and pulleys cracked and clacked in the breeze, and men shouted to one another over the crash of the waves against the hull.

I rose stiffly and sent the rats scuttling into a hole in the cabin wall. I opened the door and cold spray hit me in the face like a slap with a wet fish. My ma was standing by the steering oar at the stern, looking at a yellowed chart and talking to the steersman.

"When we've passed Lands End, head east-north-east," she was saying.

I said, "Hello, Ma!" and waited to see her scarred face burst into a smile like sunshine. She turned. Her face was as grey as a thundercloud and twice as dangerous. "What are you doing here, you idiot child?" she screamed.

"Doing what *you* did, Ma! Going off to sea to be a pirate," I said. I tried to sound cheerful, but my voice was shaking.

"I'm not having you eating the food or drinking the water that my crew need. I'm not having you getting under our feet when we fight. I'm not having you bring bad luck to this voyage," she said sternly.

"I won't, Ma," I croaked and I felt tears bubbling behind my eyes.

Ma turned to a passing sailor. "Throw this child overboard."

"But, Ma –" I began to wail, as the man strode towards me. His hand touched my wet leather jerkin and I wriggled away.

I jumped down onto the main deck and headed for the mast. The crew stopped work to watch the fun as the pirate stalked after me.

Ropes hung down from the mainsail and I gripped one. I hauled myself up and felt the sailor's hand on my shoe. I pulled upwards and the shoe came away in his hand, but at least I was free.

I kept climbing till I reached a small platform — the crow's nest — at the top of the mast. In the wind it swayed like a willow tree. I clung on tight.

"You'll come down when you're cold or hungry enough," Ma snarled. "Or you'll fall asleep and drop into the sea."

"Ma-a-a-a!" I sobbed. "You wouldn't throw your own daughter into the sea. You wouldn't!"

I don't know if she really would. I'll never know. Maybe she was just trying to frighten me, to teach me a lesson. But the mast shook in the wind, and I slipped off the platform. I reached out and felt a rope. I held it with hands as tight as a hare-hound's jaws. As I flapped around like a fish in a basket, I looked out over the sea. "Sail!" I cried. "I see a sail. Another ship!"

Ma ordered a small sailor, "Get up there and see what it is."

The man climbed like a monkey. He pushed me roughly back up into the crow's nest and joined me.

"English cog!" he shouted. "Trade ship.

Slow and low in the water. Fully loaded, I'd say, Ma'am. North by north-west, I reckon."

"Crew to attack stations!" Ma roared.

Men raced across the deck to haul out the cannon and collect weapons. The monkey-man helped me down to the deck.

My cold swim was forgotten.

Chapter Four
Whiskers and Warships

Ma had a black flag hauled to the top of our mast. It was a sign to the other ship to stop or die.

The crew of the English ship lowered their sail. They knew it was no use trying to outrun us – they were too slow. They stood at the side rails and stared, sullen and afraid.

"I'm Grace O'Malley," Ma called across, "the greatest pirate that ever lived. We are coming alongside. We will take a share of your goods and not harm you," she promised. "What are you carrying?"

"Linen and woollen cloth. A little silk," an English sailor called back.

Ma grinned at me. "Silk, Catherine. You'll have a new dress when we get home."

"So you're not going to throw me in the sea?"

She shrugged. "Only if the ship is too crowded," she joked. At least, I think it was a joke.

It took most of the morning to carry the bales of cloth across. Slowly, the English ship grew lighter and rose, and ours sank lower. When the last of the cloth was on board, the cog sailed back to Plymouth and we turned around slowly.

Our ship was riding in the water like a fallen tree. "We'll be in Dublin this time tomorrow," Ma told the crew. "Our prize will fetch a good price in the market. And we didn't even have to sail to Spain."

A small man with the face of a mouse and a thin, whiskery beard stepped forward. I knew he was Seaman Michael Paterson. "Three cheers for Captain Grace O'Malley, Pirate Queen of Ireland. Hip, hip – "

"Ship ahead!" came a cry from the crow's nest.

The cheer from the crew died in their throats.

"We haven't room below deck to take any more loot," Ma called back. "Let it go."

"It's an English warship, Captain Grace. And it's heading this way," the lookout called.

"Set sail for Ireland!" Ma cried, and the crew raced to raise the sails. But now we were low in the water and heavy with that cloth. We were as slow as the cog we'd just robbed.

The English warship drew closer and we could see her sailors loading the cannon on the decks.

"What do we do, Captain?" Paterson moaned. "They have twenty guns, we have six. They'll blow us out of the water."

Grace O'Malley wrapped a large arm around his shoulder and grinned. "No, they won't, Seaman Paterson. No, they won't. Gather round, crew – I have a plan. After all, I *am* the greatest pirate that ever lived."

"Gather round, crew!" Paterson shouted. "Captain O'Malley has a wonderful plan to save us all."

When the sailors gathered on the deck, my ma spoke quietly over the sound of the slapping waves. "Now, lads, we're in a tight spot. But we're still alive. If we stand and fight, we'll probably die. So what I think we should do is surrender."

"No-o-o-o," Paterson moaned. "They'll take us back to Plymouth and hang us all. I'd rather die fighting."

Grace O'Malley shook her head. "These are English sailors, Michael. They have a way of doing things. It's the way of gentlemen. If we raise a white flag, they won't fire on us. Their captain will come on board and he will ask me to hand over my sword as a sign that we surrender."

"Then they'll take us on their ship and hang us."

"That is the gentleman's way," Grace nodded. "But we are not gentlemen. At least, *I'm* not."

The crew chuckled. "So what do we do?"

"When their captain climbs aboard our ship, we capture him. We say we'll cut his throat if they don't let us sail home to Dublin."

"Grace O'Malley, you're not just the greatest pirate in Ireland," Paterson laughed.

"No, no, no, Michael," grinned Ma. "I'm the greatest pirate the world has ever seen!"

Chapter Five
Flag and Fall

Ma told me to climb the mast and fasten a white flag at the top. Then I was to climb back down and hide in the cabin while our crew fought the English.

I tied the flag around my neck so my hands were free to climb. Before I reached the top, I saw the English sailors loading their cannon. The knot on the flag around my neck was tangled and my cold fingers were too numb to untie it.

First I saw a puff of grey smoke from the mouth of an English cannon. Moments later, I heard the sound of the explosion and then the splash as it landed in the water just in front of our bow.

"They missed," I muttered and suddenly the flag came free.

"Hurry up, child," Ma roared at me. "That was a warning shot. The next one will hit the mast and it'll be the end of you!"

"Wait!" I cried to the English ship, but my words were whipped away by the wind.

Ma waved a fist at me. "You, Catherine O'Malley, are a disgrace to the O'Malley name!"

"Sorry, Ma," I moaned, as I wrestled with the flapping flag.

"You're as much use as a comb on a bald man's head."

"I know, Ma," I muttered, as the flag at last flew free and fluttered in my face. I clung onto the crow's nest and watched as an Englishman in a fine red coat with golden buttons stepped onto the deck of the enemy ship.

"I am Captain Dudley of Her Majesty Queen Elizabeth's fleet," the man shouted over the whipping water.

"Good for you," Ma snorted.

"I'm going to cross to your ship and take your sword as a sign of your surrender," he went on as the English frigate lowered its sails and let the wind drift it towards our side. I climbed halfway down the mast, till I was just over my ma's head.

I heard her speak softly to the crew, "He'll get my sword all right – in the throat, if I have my way."

Old Hugh O'Neil stepped forward. "Kill Captain Dudley and they'll blow us out of the water," he warned. "We need to take him prisoner, then they won't dare fire on us."

"I know that, I know that, old man," Ma snapped.

Everyone on the ship seemed to hold their breath as the English sailors threw a rope with a hook onto our deck and fastened our ships together.

They placed a plank between the ships and we watched as the English captain climbed onto our ship.

The Englishman was so fat the buttons on his red coat were bursting. But I wasn't looking at the gleaming gold buttons so much as the polished pistol he held in his hand.

"We've been waiting years to capture you, Grace O'Malley," he said. "Queen Elizabeth has heard of your evil robbing ways."

"Is that right?" Ma laughed. "What an honour for me to be so popular with old Queen Bess."

"Hand over your sword," Captain Dudley said, and jabbed his pistol towards her.

I could see Ma's plan would never work. If she tried to jump at him with her sword, he would fire his pistol and kill her. Then I remembered the tale she'd told in the draughty hall of the castle. I was clinging to the mast, just above his pistol arm.

I let go and fell towards him.

At that very moment, Ma decided to make a grab for the captain's pistol. She jumped forward. Dudley jumped back. I landed on Ma's head. She fell forward and cracked her head on the deck. She gave a soft groan and the light in her eyes went out.

Chapter Six
Richmond and Ruffs

The English captain had my ma carried across to his ship. Seaman Michael Paterson jumped forward and pushed his mouse face close to Captain Dudley. I thought he was going to fight and die for Ma.

But he just whined, "Oh, Captain, sir, we are so very happy to be free of the pirate queen! We've been her slaves for years."

The rest of the black-hearted crew began to nod and agree to Paterson's lies.

"Let us go free," the little seaman snuffled. "We'll go back to our old mothers and our weeping wives. We'll never set foot on a pirate ship again. If we do, you can cut off the feet that touch the decks. Isn't that right, lads?"

"Aye," they agreed.

Captain Dudley looked around and his long, fine nose sniffed the air as if he were smelling rats. He was. "It's Grace O'Malley we want. I haven't room on my ship to arrest the lot of you. Clear off back to Ireland."

The crew hurried across the decks to set sail for freedom. I ran after Captain Dudley. "I want to go with my ma!" I told him.

The man just shrugged and nodded.

Ma was fastened in chains and put in the captain's cabin. She woke as we set sail along the coast of England. "What happened?" she muttered, rubbing her head.

"Something fell on top of you," I said.

Before she could ask, the cabin door opened and Captain Dudley walked in. "Well, Grace O'Malley, Queen Elizabeth herself has asked to see you before we hang you. The Queen of England wants to meet the Queen of the Pirates."

"It's a great honour," Ma said coldly. "An honour for Elizabeth, that is," she added.

"We'll be at Tilbury dock tomorrow morning," said the man. "Here's some bread and cheese for you and the girl." Then he left.

Ma grinned. "Not just bread and cheese, Catherine, my dear. But a knife to cut it with. A knife I plan to plunge into the heart of Queen Elizabeth, if the woman has a heart."

"No, Ma! They'll kill you if you try."

"They plan to hang me anyway," she argued. "I may as well take that Tudor witch with me."

And nothing I could say would change her mind.

Ma had slipped the knife into her boot, and next day we rattled over the rutted roads of London to Greenwich Palace. Crowds were waiting at the gate.

"They've come to see the greatest pirate in the world," Ma laughed, and waved at the people.

We were led across a courtyard and through a door that was big enough to make a Connacht ship. The hall was crowded with gentlemen in satin jackets of more colours than a rainbow and ruffs as big as cartwheels. The ladies were in silk but in dull shades of brown and black.

Ma leaned towards me and whispered, "See? The queen doesn't like ladies to shine brighter than her."

"No, Ma," I said.

We stood in front of an empty throne and Ma looked around. "Have you all had a good look, you English peacocks?" she shouted. "You can tell your children you've seen the greatest pirate in the world."

Suddenly, a door behind the throne opened and the people in the court bowed very low. The Queen of England walked in.

Chapter Seven
Teeth and Tales

Queen Elizabeth walked slowly. Her ugly face was painted white, and red powder was brushed on her lips and cheeks. Her little black eyes glittered like wet coal and she hobbled under the weight of her dress, which was crusted with jewels.

While everyone except Ma had their heads bowed to the floor, I dropped to my knees. With a quick flick,

I'd raised Ma's skirt and pulled the knife out of her boot.

Queen Elizabeth frowned. "You should curtsey before your queen."

Ma gave a secret smile and bent her knees in a deep curtsey. I watched as she swept back her hand and felt in her boot for the knife. Her hand jerked upwards and she cried out, "Aieeee!", her killing scream.

She looked at the empty hand. She blushed. She gave a giggle. "Er... I... er... eeee... er... oh, my knees... my *knees*. The old bones hurt these days," she mumbled, to cover her foolish cry.

The English queen nodded. "I know, my dear, I have the same problem. My doctor gives me some good ointment made from goose grease. I'll get my maids to fetch you some."

"It will be a great comfort when you hang me from the gallows tomorrow."

Elizabeth looked at Ma, curious. "So you're the pirate I've heard so much about."

"And you're the queen I've heard a bit about. You're not very tall, are you?"

I heard a gasp from the crowd at my ma's cheek. The old queen smiled and showed black and broken teeth. "I haven't got my father's massive body, but I do have his huge heart, Grace O'Malley, and that's what counts in a queen. You should know that."

Ma nodded. "That's true, Bess," she said.

No one in the room seemed to breathe.

"How did you get into the pirate trade?" the queen asked. She sat on her throne and patted her ginger wig straight. "Sit by my side and tell me."

Ma moved to the seat by the throne and began her old tale. "It all started with my father. A big, bullying brute of a man."

"Same as my father... King Henry the Eighth... though we used to call him Henry the *Ate*, he grew so fat!"

For the rest of that morning, my ma told her tales of piracy and the fights she'd had. The queen asked some questions, but mostly she listened like a child at the feet of her nurse.

When the midday sun shone high in the sky, we were led off to a small room at the side of the throne room to eat. And at the end of the day, the weary old queen said, "It has been a pleasure to meet you, Grace."

Ma sighed. "And it will be your pleasure to hang me in the morning."

"Hang you? Goodness me, no! The sign of a great queen is this – you should know when to be cruel and when to show mercy.

And I am showing mercy to you, Grace O'Malley. Go back to Ireland and your family."

Ma blinked. "You're setting me free?"

"I am," Old Queen Bess said with a smile. "Rest here tonight and I'll have a ship sail you back to Connacht tomorrow."

Chapter Eight
Freedom and Feathers

Ma gave the queen a wide smile. "You really do have a heart as big as a horse."

The queen limped to the door, stopped and looked back. "Of course, if I catch you attacking any more English ships, I'll hang you from the tallest tree in Ireland."

"Of course," Ma said. "What about Spanish and Scottish ships?"

"Oh, help yourself to those!" Elizabeth chuckled. She waved a pale hand wrapped in a cloud of jewels and was gone.

Ma ruffled my hair. "She's not such a bad old bird, after all."

"No, Ma."

"In fact, I'm rather glad I didn't kill her when I had the chance."

"Me too, Ma."

"I wonder what in the devil's name happened to that knife?" she muttered.

I felt the blade hard under the back of my belt where I'd pushed it. "I wonder, Ma."

Servants led the way to a fine room in the palace and I climbed into the soft, goose-feather bed next to my ma.

"I like this," she said as she lay back sleepily. "Maybe we'll rob a ship that has a goose-feather bed on board, eh, Catherine?"

"No, Ma, you need to give up pirating," I moaned. "If the Spanish catch you, they won't forgive you like Queen Bess did."

Ma gave a long sigh. "You're right, Catherine, you're right. But it would be a terrible pity to retire when I'm the greatest pirate the world has ever seen."

"Yes, Ma," I said, and fell asleep in the arms of the greatest ma the world has ever seen.

Epilogue

In this story Catherine is made up. Grace O'Malley (born around 1530) was real. She was the Pirate Queen of Connacht with three galleys and 200 warriors. She cut her hair short so she could sail with her father. That's probably how she got her nickname Granuaile, which means "bald".

Her father always refused to let her sail with him, so she had to hide on one of his ships. Her first husband, Donal, was a pirate on the west coast of Ireland. When he died, she took over his fleet of ships.

She was hated by the English, who ruled Ireland, and they set out to arrest her.

Grace also took over her second husband's castle. She was trapped there by an English army. She took lead from the roof, melted it and poured the boiling lead on the English heads to drive them away. When her father died, she took over his fleet, too. She began to raid England and Scotland as well as Ireland.

In 1593, she went to London to meet Queen Elizabeth. The two women were about the same age – around 60 – when they met at Greenwich Palace.

Grace wore a fine gown, but had a dagger hidden on her person. Guards found it before she could attack the queen. Grace said she was carrying the dagger to defend herself. Queen Elizabeth believed her.

Grace refused to bow before Elizabeth because, she said, Elizabeth wasn't the Queen of Ireland. Still, Elizabeth liked Grace O'Malley and set her free. Grace said she would stop her rebel raids and Elizabeth said she would stop the English soldiers attacking Grace's castles. But Grace broke her promise and soon went back to her wicked ways.

Both women died in the year 1603.

TERRY DEARY'S VIKING TALES

The Eye of the
VIKING God

The Hand of the
VIKING Warrior

The Sword of the
VIKING King

The Battle of the
VIKING Woman